MW01229108

LIFE AFTER DEATH

AN AUTOBIOGRAPHY

ADAM J PITKANEN

 FriesenPress

Suite 300 - 990 Fort St
Victoria, BC, V8V 3K2
Canada

www.friesenpress.com

Copyright © 2017 by Adam J Pitkanen
First Edition — 2017

All rights reserved.

No part of this publication may be reproduced in any form, or by any means, electronic
or mechanical, including photocopying, recording, or any information browsing,
storage, or retrieval system, without permission in writing from FriesenPress.

ISBN
978-1-4602-9734-6 (Hardcover)
978-1-4602-9735-3 (Paperback)
978-1-4602-9736-0 (eBook)

1. FICTION, CHRISTIAN

Distributed to the trade by The Ingram Book Company

AFTER DEATH

There was the sound of a monitor quietly beeping next to my head. The walls around my small room were bare except for this gold crucifix hanging over the window and a TV hanging off to the side but within reach of the bed. Around me I recognized the faces of people that I loved. Some, with tears in their eyes, now looked down at me as if I were stuck at the bottom of a far and deep well.

My wife was sitting to my right and a soft whisper of reassurance left her lovely lips to touch my ears and my heart. "It'll be fine, love."

My son stood on my left. He's so grown up I can barely believe that only seventeen years earlier I held him in my arms with tears flowing down my cheeks. Now he stood holding my hand with tears falling down his.

My family had come to be with me because I would never again see them in life. This was our goodbye. I moved my mouth to speak, but only a gurgle and a squeak seemed to escape my throat. My mind had so much to say. To give words of comfort for my parents who had lived to see me die. To my brother who had come back to us. One last "I love you" was all I wanted to say.

My mother placed her hand on my leg and smiled down at me. "We know, and we love you too."

I looked to my right, to my wife – my lover. With tears in her eyes she touched my face and said, "It's ok, love. You don't have to fight anymore." She wiped away the tears from my cheek and her eyes spoke of all the love she had for me. Of our first date and the time she'd laughed so hard at one of my lame and sarcastic jokes that she ended up with a nose full of water. Our first Christmas and the last time we made love. Our story was in her eyes.

I mouthed *I love you* to her, and I turned to my son. I didn't want this for him. I didn't want him to be at my side and to have to endure this. I wanted to be able to see him walk across the stage at graduation and to see him move on to college and find the love of his life. I wanted to be his father on his wedding day, to secretly shed tears when my little boy said, "I do." I wanted to hold my grandchild and hear my son say, "Here's Grandpa." I tried to say how proud I was of him. How much I loved him. I wanted to say everything to him in that moment that I'd never thought of saying when I could. Why didn't I? Why didn't I take those few precious minutes to say that I would always be there for him? Maybe it's because I knew that wasn't true.

My son, my precious son looked into my eyes and

said, "It's ok, Dad. I love you so much. You have made me who I am today. You have made me the man I am. I love you so much. You taught me to stand for what's right and how to love no matter what. I know that you will always be here, in my heart."

Tears flowed freely. With all my strength I brought my hand to my mouth still clutching on to my son's. Tenderly I kissed his hand. I heard my last breath leave my lungs and then light began to fade. The faces of my loved ones disappeared and into the darkness I entered. I was numb and cold but at peace.

It felt like only seconds had passed, and then in the darkness there was a bright light. I thought to myself, *Oh you gotta be kidding me!* Out of all of the stories one hears of life after death; of angels or of seeing St. Peter at the gate of Heaven, the one I get is a long, dark tunnel with a light at the end. Well, if this is my experience then I'm going to go at it full force! *Run to the light!* I told myself over and over. The more I ran towards it the farther the stupid light got. I found myself thinking that maybe I was going backwards, but all the warning signs in my heart told me not to turn around. The story of Job's wife, who looked back and was turned into a pillar of salt, came to my mind. Maybe this was the last test to know if you were worthy of Heaven. "Eyes forward, mister," came the voice of my scary grade-four teacher. "Focus on your goal," came the voice of my one-time swim coach.

Eyes forward and focused I just kept heading towards the light at the end of this dark tunnel. The numbness that had surrounded me at death seemed to be melting away, and there was warmth that started to grow around me. It was as if my wife was gradually adjusting the thermostat even though she knew that bugged me to all get-up. The space around me seemed to grow smaller and I realized that the infinite amount of empty space, which had once made me feel like I was floating, was now removed, and in fact I felt now that gravity was pulling me into the light. Every episode of *Star Trek* and *Star Wars* that involved the use of the tractor beam was now flashing through my mind, and so was that famous line of Mr. Scott's: "That's all she's got an I can't git no more Cap't," in his famously overdone Scottish accent. I laughed at myself. Only I would find something like that to laugh about in a moment like this. I'm such a nerd. I think that's what made my wife love me so much.

I passed into the light.

Everything was lost to me. I couldn't hear anything, but I knew that I was naked. I heard voices all around me, but my sight was blurred and I couldn't make out things around me. There were shapes but nothing that I could figure out. It was colder but maybe that's because I was naked.

I got wrapped in a blanket and laid down on a soft, bed-like area. I was glad to know that I had been a

Christian in life, because I was pretty sure that I was now lying on a cloud. I tried to say something but words weren't coming to me. I tried to move around, but my blanket was so heavy. My sight was still blurred and my hearing seemed muted. I waited in silence, slowly allowing myself to drift off on this cloud of heavenly comfort.

Some time went by and I was awoken by the sound of someone saying my name. The voice said, "Adam. Hello there, Adam."

My eyes were stuck together with sleep, but as I opened them it was like coming out of a really dark tunnel into a summer's day. There was a face not far from my own. It took a few seconds, but the blur started to fade and I found my eyes focussing on a very familiar face. I couldn't explain it. I didn't know what was going on, but I knew this shouldn't be happening.

I looked around for someone else and saw yet another face, this one standing off to the side. I recognised that face as well and now knew that something wasn't right. *I must be dreaming. This must be some kind of morphine-induced dream.* I closed my eyes again – shut hard. On my opening them I found the two faces were still there with wide smiles from ear to ear. I tried to speak but I didn't know what words to say. A noise came out, but it was more like a pathetic coo. The smiles grew bigger and I saw a tear building in the eye of the second face.

"Adam Jason," said the first face.

"Yeah, he's definitely Adam Jason," said the second.

I went to reach out for the first face but found myself still weighed down by the heavy blanket they had placed on me when I'd first arrived. How could this be?

"That's your name, sweetheart: Adam Jason Pitkanen," said the first face – my mother's.

My father, who stood beside her, said, "Welcome, little guy."

I started to grasp the surroundings around me and saw that I was in a hospital room. I saw that the soft pillow I had mistaken for a cloud was my mother's chest, and that I couldn't move my arms because I was swaddled.

I had just been born again. Not the way that Christ speaks of but in a totally new and unknown way to me. And why did I still have the memories of my past life? How did this work? My parents looked young. Much younger than at the last moment I had seen them. The grey was gone from their heads, and the extra weight seemed to have melted off. Lines and wrinkles were gone, which I had come to know as scars of victories in battles fought between my brother and me while we were growing up. They both wore smiles that I'd never seen on their faces. It must have been like that for me the day my son came into my life.

My son…what has happened to my son if I am here as a child? Did he live a full life? Did he even exist? I closed my eyes tight to try and wake myself up but when I opened them again all I saw were the same two faces staring intently at mine. Sadness seemed to take me— images of my son and my wife danced in my mind. I started to cry and the sound I heard scared me. The voice I heard was coming from my body was a baby's. No words came out—just noise.

My dad looked concerned and frantically asked my mom what she had done. Mom looked at him and half laughed/half rolled her eyes. "Arne," she said, "he's hungry that's all. It's nothing to worry about."

He's what?! Did I just hear her say that she thought I was hungry? No, no, no, this would not be good. I knew, as does anyone who has brought up a child, what and where a baby eats. I didn't want to go there at all. Let's just say that this moment was going to mean that I would need to go under intensive counselling as a teenager. I struggled at first to keep those things away from me. I mean come on! Then I realized that if this was reality then I needed to eat and this was how it worked. So I allowed myself to get something to eat, but I made a mental note to try to make that happen as little as possible. I chuckled and thought, *Well, at least I get to crap anywhere and anytime and I don't have to clean it!* That would become my new game. Where was the worst place I could poop? If I was to be stuck in that baby body, then I was going to have fun.

I thought of my son again and wondered if this would happen to him when he died—if this was something that happened to everyone, and if the ideas of Heaven or Hell or reincarnation were all just muffled images of this. That we aren't reborn into other's lives and other's bodies but just replay our lives over and over again like that movie, *Groundhog Day* with Bill Murray. I hated that movie but came to a realisation that this could be my Groundhog Day. I had already lived a life, and so now I could relive it stopping things that were bad and doing things that I knew I would love to do. This was a second chance to live a life without fear or at least with a heads-up in certain areas. I would know things before they would happen. All of a sudden I wished I had paid more attention to winning lotto numbers. I could stop things like September 11th from ever happening, or stop my friend from dying in a car accident when she was sixteen. I could tell the people who I knew would end up with cancer that they were going to get it and save them. I could not get sick...I could save myself.

I didn't realise it until after my thought process had died down, but I had fallen asleep. My eyes were tightly closed and I was breathing slowly. I stopped thinking and let sleep take my mind.

As time went by it became frustratingly clear that although my memories were intact, I was still limited by the process of being a baby. I had parents who were first-time parents and didn't understand certain things. As if through a two-way mirror, I sat by witnessing the mistakes that made me cringe as a parent myself.

I watched with panic as my mom and dad were faced with trying to discover if I had inherited my dad's epilepsy. It felt almost like torture knowing that I hadn't but being unable to tell them. My dad was the one who seemed the most affected by that thought. It wasn't something he wished on his worst enemy let alone his son.

At one of the many bath times I had, my dad swore that I rolled my eyes at him. To be honest I did. Trying to put up with his jokes later on in life was hard, but not being able to respond with an, "Oh Dad," made rolling my eyes the only option I had left.

I constantly tried to make noises. Not crying but trying to get my mouth to make words. All of a sudden the whole baby talk thing made total sense to me. I thought at one point that I had managed to finally speak English and had my mom's complete attention. She nodded and grinned and made me, the older me behind the mask I wore, feel really dumb once I came to realise she was just playing along. I gave her the cold shoulder for that trick. It didn't last long, though, because I know that on more than one occasion I'd done the same thing with my son; the son I was to have one day in the future.

Having these memories tore my mind apart in the quiet dark that I seemed trapped in. I longed for my wife and my son. I wanted to smell her hair and to go to his first swim meet. I reminded myself that it would happen. *I'll get to do that all over again.* I just would have to wait a couple of decades first.

I found TV really interesting the first few years of my life. The little that I saw was usually news. To relive some of those things in history seemed amazing in my mind. They talked a lot about the Hitler diaries and the death of the first heart-transplant recipient after only 120 days.

My first word came early. I was finally able to utter a word at nine months. The look on my parents' face was shock and a little disappointment. My first word was Alexander, my son's name. It was the mystery of the ages for them because we knew no Alexanders. My dad thought that maybe it was something I'd heard on a tape or something, but I would never be able to explain that to them.

The first moment I uttered my son's name I knew that I had already altered the life I had. I was going to change my world and make life as amazing as possible.

I was already walking by the time I was able to say my first word. Let's just say the farther my head was from the ground the better in my mind. My parents boasted about how advanced their child was. I figured hey, no harm in making them proud of me and of themselves. Felt like I was cheating a bit, but hey, if you had inside information at a track race you'd be an idiot not to use it, right? As soon as I was walking I was pooping and peeing without that stupid diaper. The thought of being lazy had been nice at first. The smell and the feeling are not all that pleasant. Not to mention I learned why they circumcise at a young age. If a baby could describe that pain to you there is no way that the practice of cutting off that skin would be continued. Its initial stuff is painful but the aftermath is unbearable. I knew it was coming and when I overheard that conversation between my mom and dad I remember bursting out in tears. It got a funny reaction out of them in the moment. Both looked at me as if they were trying to figure out if I understood what they were talking about.

I have to admit part of the fun of having this experience was that I could mess with them. My dad was my favourite of the two targets. Once I had control of my motor skills, finding something to put between his sandwiches was always a blast. I once found a discarded wet nap and left it nicely hidden in the middle of his tuna sandwich. I don't know if you've ever pranked anyone, but the watching is the fun part. Dad brought the sandwich up to his mouth and was about to chomp down when my mom called him. He put it down and went to her aid, leaving me alone. Two minutes later he came back, checked on me, and then chomped down. His first bite had a mouth full of wet nap. He pulled it out and it dangled from his mouth. He sat there wide-eyed and staring at me as I cackled my baby butt off. He tried to convince my mom that I had done it, but there was no convincing her that I could do something like that at just under a year old.

At one I was speaking full sentences but held back so as to not make people look at me and get too weird. I figured that if I was too fluent too young, I would end up in some lab where they'd be trying to decipher what made me so special.

The place we lived in was small, but I didn't mind. In fact, it made me realise that later on in life when I had a child of my own that it would have been nice to start off in something close and intimate like this shack of a house was.

Just after my first birthday my mother one day sat down in front of me on the floor. In my eyes she is and always will be a beautiful woman, but I saw her in a new way from behind my two-way mirror. Maybe it was just the youth in her that I had seen drained later on in life. I walked to her and said the cutest baby line I could think of. She smiled, opened her arms to me, and embraced me as I closed into her. She looked me in the eyes and talked really low as if to keep other people from hearing her, although it was just she and I in the house. She said, "Adam, you have eyes that are full of an unknown wisdom and I don't know where you've gotten it from." She paused almost as if she were able to discern that I had a secret that I wasn't telling her. I honked her nose. She smiled at me and then laughed. "Well there goes that assumption." Later on in life honking her nose always got me out of a serious talk.

Before letting me go she looked deeper than ever into my eyes and asked me straight out as if I would answer her: "Adam, why was your first word Alexander?"

I said, "Mommy," and honked her nose again.

She let out a sigh, placed me on the ground, and got up and went about making dinner. I had thought about if I would ever tell either of my parents about what was really going on in my mind. I came to the conclusion that it would be the best for me to not say anything. I didn't know why I had been given this chance again, but for some reason I knew that I needed to keep that secret to myself. Besides that, if I went around proclaiming that I was a forty-eight-year-old man in the body of an infant I might be locked away or studied for my entire life. I had things to do and people to save. Most of all I was here to save me. My secret was to be kept; only I would ever know.

"It's the big day! Are you ready?" asked my dad. It was the day of my brother's birth. This may sound odd but I looked forward to this more than anything else so far. Frankly I had been getting bored lately. I was now two and able to speak a lot more without raising eyebrows. I'm glad I love to act because I had to do a lot of it while in public. I remember being put in nursery situations and thinking, *Where's a good book when you need one*? I once read a newspaper three times over while the negligent steward was paying attention to the kids at the play-dough station, and I stayed off in the distance, just out of sight. At home this was easier for me to accomplish because my dad enjoyed reading the paper, so my parents thought I was just copying him. If they'd known that I was reading about the assassination of Indira Gandhi or how Reagan was making all the right choices, I may have had some explaining to do. Having a brother would, if anything, give me some more freedom to get away with not having their constant gaze on me. Besides, I also knew that we were moving soon, really soon. I was surprised that somehow my parents mainly managed to talk about the new house when I wasn't around. I assume they put me to bed and went and had their discussions then.

That year marked the arrival of Jonathan and the home my parents would live in up until the day I died. That was a weird thought. Until the day I died. I wondered at times if I told them my secret and of everything that would yet come whether they would even believe me. And if they did would they be able to live with that? Would telling them change things right then and there?

The move was the easiest move I've ever been a part of. They gave me my plush animals to move in, so with arms full of stuffed fluff balls I proudly walked into my home; the home I had known my entire previous life. On my way into the house I was accidentally knocked over by an adult who turned around and snipped, "Watch it!" My biggest slip-up came at this point. I dropped a curse at that man. My parents did not swear and none of the families I was around in my life ever did. Dropping "a-hole" loud enough for the man to hear was a big mistake. I thought maybe I was lucky and he was too busy to really hear it, but when I noticed this tall shadow behind me, standing motionless as if stunned, I knew that he'd caught that a two-year-old had just cursed at him. I tried to make a break for it, but he grabbed my shirt faster than I thought he could move. In my mind I had a few other choice words for this guy.

He took me over to Mom, who was holding baby Jonathan, and he held me up like I had a dirty diaper on. He told me to repeat what I'd just said. I looked at my mom and said, "I want an apple." The man holding me didn't know what to do or to say at this point. He wasn't sure if I had said apple or the other, and he now slowly put me down on the ground. I looked at him and said, "Why were you angry? Is apples bad fo me?"

He knelt down on a knee so that he made eye contact with me and said that he was sorry. Leaving me at my mom's side, he walked away. Mom, of course, was pre-occupied, so I was able to sneak off.

I found my way into my dad's tools and found his crazy glue. I undid the lid just enough so that if someone happened to, for example, sit on it, the lid would come off. I then went and found the man's vehicle. It being 1985, no one had yet even thought of having to lock your car door, so I opened it and placed the tube at the back of his seat. I don't know if that ever worked. All I know is that while I watched from the window, innocently waving goodbye as he got into his car, he didn't seem to move anything. He sat down and drove off. Later that month, Dad was looking for his tube of crazy glue to fix something he'd broken before Mom saw it, but that was the last I heard of it.

The next few years were tedious for me. I was constantly acting my part. I let certain things happen that I knew were supposed to happen. Like the surgery I had on my throat. I still couldn't figure out what that was all about. I listened but nothing made a lot of sense. I acted so strong. In my previous life my experience with hospitals had been really extensive, so I took it like a champ. Nurses and doctors alike were amazed with how for a three-year-old I was so calm and almost nonchalant about it. IVs were put in and I just shrugged it off. They were more painful than they would be when I was older in life, but my mind told me that was because my skin had never experienced it before. I didn't give anyone the satisfaction of seeing me cry. Besides, I think I got extra popsicles because I was so brave.

The surgery and everything around it happened just like it had the first time. Having a baby brother turned out to be more of a pain than a blessing. I loved him and part of me was wondering if what was happening to me was happening to him. But if it had taken me all that time to get motor control, then I knew he would take time. I remember looking into his eyes to see if I could see the depth and age that my mom had once seen in mine. He just cooed and pooed a lot. My time alone with him was very limited, but I was convinced that I would have to find some time to test my theory of everyone just recycling their lives.

The moment finally came that I had time to talk to him. My mom was busy on the phone and had left him in the baby bouncer. I walked up to him and quietly started talking as adultly as I could. "Ok, listen. I need to know if you understand me. I know you can control your head and neck so give me a nod if you're following me," I said in my hushed toddler voice. I don't know if it was the baby bouncer or if he nodded, and I didn't know if I had more time or not. I looked deep into his eyes and said, "I know you feel trapped in there, Jonathan. Nod your head. Blink your eyes give me a sign that you are the adult-you in there."

I know that there was no reaction. By his age I had been able to control the body enough to give a pur-posed thumbs-up or a peace sign. As I walked away he started to giggle and scream with delight. I turned quickly to see if this was his reaction to what I had said. Mom had just come back into view. I was alone.

Kindergarten kind of came with mixed blessings for me. I was glad to be getting out of the house—more than I thought I would be. The idea of at least being around other people excited me. This was my chance to be the king of Riverside Elementary. I was going to be the cool one. This was finally the time that I could start my do-over life.

Things happened just like they had before. Mom enrolled me in the French immersion program and my teacher was the same as my first time at bat. We met the same people as we had the first time. The only thing I changed was to freak out my teacher. My schooling was still strongly engraved in my mind, and I decided that it would be fun to know more French than what she was teaching. After my mom left, I went right up to her and started singing her welcoming song in French to her. Slack-jawed, she looked at me and then around the room. Maybe she was hoping there was some other adult in the room to verify what had just happened. I'd already made sure there wasn't. I walked away and then she did her thing and gathered all the students together—all the while looking at me as if I had done something she had never seen coming. My first day was great.

My second day was even better because when the teacher called on me to sing the welcoming song in French, I looked at her with a puzzled look on my face and said, "Teacher, I don't know that song yet, you haven't taught it to me." My parents got a call that night to see if I had an older sibling or if they spoke French at home at all. I think she ended up chalking it all up to her imagination. She never mentioned it again; she also never called on me to ever sing the song. The thing I found that I loved the most was that there were adults there to at least listen to. Kindergarten was actually really slow. Already being fluent in French I actually found that the teacher was making mistakes, and when I thought back on it realized that she ended up teaching English the year after I was in kindergarten and never went back to French.

Maybe she realized that I had correctly done what she had done wrong when she marked me wrong. I walked over to her and asked her why and she couldn't explain except that it was how she had taught it and that her way was right. As a five-year-old I doubt I would've won that argument, so I looked at her almost with a glaring, condemning gaze and returned to my spot. It was craft time and I had to make something for Mom. It was hard to make it look like crap. I usually scoped the room and tried to judge what I would do in comparison to the other kids in my area. Mine, of course, still looked amazing in comparison, but it was at least at a closer level.

Grade one was a year that almost gave me away. First time around I'd had a huge crush on my grade one teacher, and honestly I had great taste at six or seven. She was kind and caring and loved her students. So being a man in a kid's body, I tried to show off for her. Obviously I wasn't going to win her over in looks. I was twenty years too young. So I figured I could go for being smart, and then she'd give me extra attention. I got extra attention all right, just not what I wanted. My answers were way too smart for a student in grade one. Not on math because that's just numbers. But when one finishes the entire math book, which was meant for the first half of the year, in a month, eyebrows kind of get raised. They considered skipping me a grade. That idea was intriguing at first, but then I thought it better not to. I ended up dumbing my act down. I wanted to be able to at least have a chance of changing the situations that I wanted so badly to change. It was very difficult to go from finishing all my work for the first half of the year, to "S" for satisfactory. My parents fell under the scope because administration thought that maybe there was something fishy going on at home.

Grade two was very similar. I found myself with my favourite teacher over again. She just had a way of making me feel special about myself. I was pretty popular, all the kids seemed to like me a lot, and I was a natural leader in my teacher's eyes. The one thing in that year that sucked was that I got stuck doing a Christmas pageant, and I had to wear lederhosen and sing "Oh Tannenbaum." Didn't like it the first time, didn't look forward to it this time. As my entire class walked onto the stage, one elder classmate from a different class saw us walking in and starting making fun of us right and left. He pushed each of us as we walked up the steps. When it came to my time to get pushed, I grabbed his arms and pulled as he pushed. Down the steps he went. He didn't really get hurt. I got into some trouble but not much—my classmates told the teachers I was defending everyone.

The next time I saw him he told me he was suing me. I told him to go for it. Sue away. You can have the whole twenty-five cents I have. He really didn't know what to say about that. I found it sad. First time around he had been my biggest struggle. I mean, this time around I had my mom put me in soccer and swimming at a much earlier age. I started doing push-ups and sit- ups as a routine really early. I didn't want to end up that pudgy little kid that got picked on. Not this time. I wouldn't let it come to that again.

Elementary was a lot more fun for me the second time around. I was constantly playing dumb with my teachers and found myself amazed when I realised how little some of these people really knew. By grade six I realized that my attitude towards some older people might have to change, due to the fact that I found myself thinking I was better and knew more than them. I laughed and realized that when Alexander was that age he'd had the same attitude. I thought of cutting back a bit but thought that most people would just see me as being a kid—just a normal pre-teen trying to act older than he was. My popularity was soaring. I knew exactly what it was that I needed to do and say to maintain that. I was well liked in all my circles. Whether in sports or at school, I found myself almost admired. Not because I did what was wrong, but because I stood for what was good. It was hard for me, though, to be as into God as I had been in my first life. My family still went to church, but after I turned nine and became old enough to look after myself, in my parents' eyes, I often found myself playing sick to get out of going. I loved singing and the people at the church, but this time around I had really hard questions to answer about life and death. My whole perception of how life works was tainted and had thrown into question the whole need for a God. If we just recycle, then why bother seeking guidance? It was on one of my "sick" days that I was sitting in front of the TV watching the *Hour of Power* and chewing over some of these questions that I had an epiphany. The thing that had made life possible the last time was church. God was the reason why I turned out the way I did the first time around. Church played such an integral part in my life that if I were to not go, the things that I wanted to happen might not.

I made an important decision that day. I was going to give it my all once more. I would pursue God in any way I could and be known as someone that loved him. Up until that point I had even bowed out of being baptised and stayed far from the spiritual side of God. My parents never pushed me as I believe they understood that it had to be my heart not theirs that would need to turn to Jesus. The next few months I dove into church and ended up re-giving my heart and life to God. I didn't know if that was needed because I had already done that in my over- extended life. I thought for a while that it would be foolish to give something that had already been given. The thought of dying and going through the entire birth process again made me realize that this life I was living was new, and I hadn't given it to God. That was the choice I made at twelve. Way later than the first time, but I thought that God would understand. The summer I was to go into grade eight I got baptised. This time I had no doubt as to what I was doing. I wanted to be God's even though there were doubts and some confusion.

High school was something that I was looking forward to. Out of all the things I wanted to have a do-over with in my life it had to be those five years of mistakes. At least this way I would know what to do when the big temptations came up. On top of that my family had switched churches. After the nine years put into the first one, my parents felt fed up with the antics that were going on so they moved us. I knew right away that I would push for a church that they didn't even know of. They wanted to attend a church in Coquitlam, but I sat down one day in front of both of them and said that I would really like to talk to them. I was trying to muster up as much "adultness" as possible. I explained to them that the idea of going to Coquitlam was cool and almost the safe bet because we knew people at the church they were aiming for, but I convinced them that God had called us as a family to be in Maple Ridge. The difficult part was that as far as I knew there had been no mention in our home of the church I wanted as of yet. Bringing it up out of the blue would have been extremely odd. It just so happened that there was a flyer sent out to the community talking about this church, and so when I saw it I grabbed it and stored it because I knew this day was coming. I handed my parents the flyer and my mom and dad looked at me as if I had read their minds but didn't know that I had. We started going there the summer of grade six (going into grade seven). It was a year early but I knew this wouldn't affect anything. This was where we were for years in my first life, so I figured why not get a jump on it. High school became something more of a side note to me. I did well in my studies, although math was still very much hated—maybe even more the second time around. I maintained my level of friends and popularity but at the same time found that what it took to be popular meant being mean, and I remembered that this time around meant that I was going to do things right. I slowly distanced myself from the taunting and cruel behaviour and kept God as my focus. Besides, my real friends were the ones I had in church. I was growing closer and closer to them as we spent more and more time together. I was easily accepted there even if they may have called me a know-it-all.

I believed that one of my purposes in this life was to help people. Because of going to the church early we were there before there was a suicide among the congregation. It was drastic and caused most of the congregation to lose heart. It hit me really hard. I had forgotten. He was such a nice guy and on the surface everything seemed so good with him. It was devastating to see the storm that was raging just below the surface, because it revealed itself in such a drastic way. I was in mourning for him, but I also was mad at myself for not stopping it. "I could have done something!" I said one day when I was surrounded by my friends.

"No, Adam none of us could have done anything," was the answer I heard from one of the girls in the youth group; one of my new friends. She didn't understand. I moved my mouth in a quick response to answer her, until the reality of my situation hit me. How was I to explain that I was in a cycle of a previous life and that this had happened the first time? Maybe stopping his death was the one and only reason I had been sent back. Maybe I had just failed my sole purpose for being back with all my memories. I still had a life to live. I still was able to remember the rest of what was to come, so I told myself that my reason for being back wasn't just this situation.

I vowed that day to always take action—to do what I could to save the people in my life from suffering and pain. I was going to become Batman. I wished it were that simple. Batman hid behind a mask and fought criminals for justice. I would be in the open, known, and the enemy I was going to try to stop wasn't a petty crook but death itself in certain circumstances. I didn't have a delusion of grandeur—I knew I was not God and that I did not have the power over life and death, but I thought maybe I could just delay it.

I spent the next few days angrily writing down the names of everyone who had died in my previous life and to the best of my ability what they had died of. I thought of situations of abuse and of people that I knew faced bad in their lives. Months later, after poring over the names, I decided it was time to approach one of the friends I thought I could help. I wouldn't be able to save her, but at least I could warn her of what was to come. We were at a church event and there had been a prophet there that specific day. I took up my courage, approached my friend, sat down next to her, and care-fully thought of what I was going to say. I looked her straight in the eye and told her that I had a word from God for her.

"What is it Adam?" she asked.

All my strength and wisdom and the experience of my last life, which I relied so heavily on throughout my new life seemed to vanish. Stumbling, I tried to say something. "I don't know how I'm supposed to say this," I started. "I feel like…" There was so much happiness in her eyes. I didn't want her to be mad. I didn't want her to cry or to think that I had gone nuts. I swallowed hard and reminded myself that this was why I thought I'd been sent back. "I feel that God wants to tell you that you are going to get cancer."

The sentence started so strongly but ended in no less than a soft whisper, almost as if I was hoping she hadn't heard what I said.

"What?" she asked in shock.

"I feel like God wants me to tell you that you will develop cancer in the years to come." I felt like I had rocks in my stomach. In my last life this girl had died of cancer at a younger age and the thought was maybe if she knew now, the doctors would catch it earlier and she would live.

It made things worse that I sat there and proclaimed that God was the one saying this through me. I have had words from God for people before, in this life and in my last, but this I knew was from my heart and from knowledge of my past.

"Who the hell do you think you are?" came a voice from behind me. The friend I had just told was staring at me with wide eyes as if I had just smacked her. Behind me stood another friend who had been eavesdropping on our conversation. "How can you say that something like that came from God?" said the angry voice.

The friend I'd tried to warn stood up with her eyes locked on me. Tears formed as my angry-voiced friend joined her and they together walked off; one crying and the other staring angrily back at me with what I'm sure were death wishes.

What was I supposed to do here?! I'd done what I thought I was supposed to do. I'd done my best to save her; to warn her of a future of hospitals and grief. I hadn't expected her to react with a kindly hug and a thank you. In fact, I'd been expecting a worst scenario to happen. I hadn't, however, expected outside interference.

The next day I was contacted by my pastor and youth pastor. They both wanted to talk about what I had told my friend. We had a meeting and I was taught what a prophetic word should be. Uplifting, loving, and encouraging were some of the words used to describe what a prophecy should hold. I sat there unwilling to defend myself. I didn't know how to defend myself. I already knew that if I quoted all the prophets of the Old Testament I would get more of a lecture and less grace. I sat, head hung low, and whispered, "I'm sorry." I was told to apologize to my friend, but my friend no longer wished to be called my friend and wanted nothing more to do with me. My friend's family left the church the next week.

In the eyes of my other friends I had now stumbled. In the eyes of my parents this was the first of such things to happen. I overheard them late one night, after I had gone to bed, discussing what was "wrong" with me. "It's so unlike him," my mom said in a low tone.

"Maybe he's not lying?" answered my dad.

"I'm not saying he's lying, it just doesn't seem like him to say anything like that."

Hearing my parents talk about me like I had just committed the most unforgivable act ever made me lose faith in what I thought my purpose was now. I'd have to wait and see what would come of my warning to my friend. The present day is what I was now forced to deal with. I felt like I had turned into a plague. People tended to avoid me at all cost. Friends who had been close now crossed the road if we were walking towards each other.

I mentioned it to my mom one night thinking she would comfort me. She looked at the floor and then to the door as if hoping someone would walk through to let her off the hook. "What do you expect Adam?"

I stood as if there was a giant spider on my lap and then, heartbroken, left to take solace in my room. This wasn't how it was supposed to all work out. I was supposed to be living the life I didn't the first time around. Then something occurred to me that hadn't ever crossed my mind thus far. What if I was crazy? I mean I'd never heard of being a forty-eight-year-old who died and was now re-living his past life. What if everything I had ever thought was this brain glitch? I stopped myself from thinking for a while. I just sat there in my room staring at the wall, which I had adorned with the faces of all my friends. It hit me that if this was a mental problem then it wasn't hurting anyone except me. I had undergone brain tests to see if I had epilepsy when I was an infant, so I assumed that if there had been a tumour or something extremely wrong it would have come up in those tests. My reality was that I had all these experiences of my past life and I had to deal with it. I was now thirteen and in high school, and I was to live my life as I had planned right from the beginning. Things concerning this "fake prophecy" would blow over eventually. I just would have to keep the ball closer to my goal and simply play defence. I came to the answer that there are simply things in this world I cannot change. Some people got cancer, and some people died of it. Not a pretty picture in the long run but it was truth.

I lived life as best I could. Being a teenager again wasn't the fun I'd thought it would be. I had the awkwardness of my first kiss. Though it was with the same girl, I found it less awkward and less memorable than the first time we'd touched. My stomach wasn't flittering with the same butterflies I'd once had. Her eyes weren't my wife's. The way she smiled didn't make me feel the way I had when my wife smiled at me. The way she spoke my name made my heart sink. It seemed pointless to me to even try and endure any kind of contact with her, because I knew simply that she wasn't my one. I knew the time and place of the first time my love would walk into my life; it was etched firmly in my mind. This girl wasn't her. Like all boys my age I found girls curious and attractive, but the lingering feeling of guilt remained every time I flirted or smiled at one. They weren't her.

The summer going into grade nine came around and I went on an outreach with my church. We ventured to a Mexican community in Hood River, Oregon. It was a great time, full of laughter and amazing God moments, but it wasn't the same experience I'd had the first time. It seemed dulled. I wasn't trying to recreate the moments minute by minute, but that was the summer I grew to really know my church friends the most. Knowing them as I did already, I didn't seem to have the same amount of bonding as the others had. I often heard comments from them like, "Wow Adam, it feels like I've known you for my entire life." It was sadly true in my mind and most of them remained the same.

My twin friends whom I had known since I was two were exactly the same as they had been my first time around, as was their older brother, from whom I kept my distance. In my first shot I'd been in awe of him and he took me under his wing. The older brother was a gentle giant at heart, but he made choices in his youth that I did not wish to follow. I made a conscious choice to do what was right this time. I chose to befriend my pastor's kid and stuck as close to him as I could. I saw the life he'd led once already and knew his example was one that I admired and even envied at times. I was still friends with the friends from my past just not as close.

When we returned home from the trip, one of the moments I was dreading the most from my past was about to happen. In my past, the gentle giant had introduced me to the world of drugs the week after returning from the outreach. We went to the same place as a group and had the same party with all the same people as the first time, but when the moment came there was nothing. He never approached me alone. He never asked me to go on a walk with him. I looked around for him and realized that he was missing. In my mind I breathed a sigh of relief thinking I had already undone one of my greater shames.

I continued to play the game of volleyball we had going when it dawned on me that he would never go alone. Frantically, I searched around me for a missing member. We were all so scattered that it was impossible to tell who was where. I left the volleyball area and started to mentally tag everyone. Then I noticed that in the distance I could see the shirt of the gentle giant. I made my way over and as I approached I noticed he wasn't alone. He sat somewhat covered by a bush across from one of my other friends. She was inhaling a huge mouthful when I walked around the corner. The shock of seeing me was enough for her to gag on the smoke she was just inhaling. Gentle Giant yelled at me, "Get the hell out of here!" I felt like my feet were glued to the ground. I had never expected to see that friend sitting there with a joint in her hand. Him yes, but not her. She was one that I considered innocent. My choice in avoiding Gentle Giant had resulted in this girl becoming a closer friend to him and in him choosing to bring her into his world. He got up as if to chase me away but paused halfway up. Behind me approaching footsteps told me that there was someone coming and coming fast. I didn't even have to turn to realize that it was my pastor's wife, who was now our youth pastor. She had a presence about her that instantly told me that she was angrier than I had seen her yet in this life. In the previous life I had been the target of that anger and disappointment; the latter being far more wounding.

The youth pastor who was now standing at my side stepped in between me and the gentle giant, who was looking at me as if I had led her to them. She turned back towards me and told me to go away. Even the forty-eight-year-old inside of me felt as if I were a child at that moment. I gulped, turned on my heels, and left as fast as possible.

The next week at youth group we had a very serious talk about rules and regulations and that there was a zero tolerance for drugs. That was the last time Gentle Giant ever came to youth group. I don't know if I did wrong in this situation or not. I do know that it was a few years later that he had stopped coming to youth group in my past, and I now thought that maybe he wouldn't have enough foundation to make it through life. I tried to talk to Gentle Giant and keep him alive in church, but my efforts seemed wasted and I gradually just let him go.

Grade nine and the first part of grade ten were not like my past at all. They were so drastically different that it made me wonder if anything was going to happen the way it had before. The fear of not having my son and wife in my life seemed to hover at the back of every thought I had. People got diagnosed with cancer and I did nothing. I knew it was coming, I saw it coming, but I did nothing. When one of the people died, I felt bad but I feared the same response I'd gotten from my friend. I justified it as, *It's life and crappy things happen.* I was never satisfied by that thought, though. I still played soccer and swam, although not in competitions. I was never one who loved the thrill of beating people, so I just did sports for fun and to keep in shape. My friends at school were just friends at school. There were some really neat people there, but I did not wish to befriend anyone to a huge degree, because I'd learned once already that the friends made in school rarely keep. Because of the feeling of guilt I had about dating, my "social" life was very slim. I went on the odd date but found that even the Christian girls I dated only wanted one thing. That one thing usually centered on some-thing of a sexual nature.

My sixteenth birthday came around and now my mind was racing. Last time I'd turned sixteen I'd almost died, and I was not going to let it happen this time. I kept swimming to keep up my strength and ate as healthy as I could. Then it happened. Two weeks after my birthday I started getting sick. It wasn't bad at first but it was starting to happen just like it had before. I was having problems breathing, and I was finding everything difficult; from swimming to walking up stairs. I went to my mom and told her that we needed to go to the hospital now.

"Adam, it's just the flu or something like it," she said.

I so wanted to spill everything I knew right then and there; to tell her my secret. This was the moment I could choose to change my life forever, or I could let myself repeat things the way they were. I firmly told her that I was going to go to the hospital with or without her. She understood that whatever was going on in my mind I was serious, so she took me. I waited for hours in the ER because I wasn't considered high risk. I was so impatient, because in my mind I knew exactly what was at risk. My mom thought I was having a panic attack.

I sat there and paced the floor back and forth until I finally lost it. "Look," I said to the nurse, "I know you are doing your job here, but I can guarantee you that I'm a higher priority than all these other people. I know what I have. It's called cardiomyopathy and I need that to be confirmed now."

The nurse looked like I was standing there in front of her with my heart pulled out of my chest and still beating in my hand while I yelled *Kalima*. My mom sat with the expression of a deer in headlights as the nurse looked from her to me.

"Ma'am, I'm not trying to be an ass, but I'm serious here. The more I wait the worse my heart is going to get."

I felt a hand on my shoulder, and there next to me was the security guard. He was a small, squat man, and I stood there debating if I could take him down if I needed to. I might not have the power to save others. I might not be even able to warn others, but I would not stand there and let myself go through all that hell that I'd gone through in the past. I would not allow myself to face death at the age of sixteen.

My mom was standing now and trying to quiet me down. Over in the nurse's direction a doctor was now standing there. "How do you know that term?" she asked. "How do you know the term cardiomyopathy?"

I stood in utter disbelief because it was the same doctor who had misdiagnosed me in my past. I didn't want this one! Any other doctor but this one! I looked her straight in the eye and said, "I know it because that's what I have, dilated cardiomyopathy."

She looked sceptical.

"No, I don't have Hepatitis B or C, I don't have a liver problem, my skin may look yellow to you, but that's because my body may be shutting down. I don't have a lung infection, although my side does hurt, but that is more or less likely due to a blood clot that is in there at this exact moment! Just take me in, hook me up to a monitor, do an ECG, take an X-ray of my chest and do blood work on all my blood enzymes and INR."

There was complete silence in the entire hospital waiting room.

I found myself in a hospital bed seconds after blowing up that way. I don't know why exactly, but they did every test I asked for. To their surprise, not mine, they found that my heart was indeed enlarged. They explained it to my mom and dad the next day, but as I knew they would, they left me out of it.

One thing was different right off the bat. I was visited by a psychiatrist while still in the ER. She asked me questions that were all to do with how I knew this or that. I was asked if I'd gone online and looked up these terms. I was asked if some other doctor had ever diagnosed me with this. She was not the best shrink I've ever duelled with. She seemed to accept the fact that I'd had a dream in which I had seen this all happen. I told her it was all just a gut feeling.

My other doctor came in my first day in the hospital. He immediately had a look of bewilderment on his mostly comforting face. He sat at the foot of my bed and looked me straight in the eye. "Adam, how did you know what to look for?" he asked, hoping for more than what I'd told Mrs. Shrink. "How did you know to ask for an ECG, INR, and heart enzymes test?"

I admired this man. I remembered attending his

funeral in the past and couldn't find the nerve in me to lie to him, so I simply shrugged my shoulders. He moved to get off the foot of the bed and I grabbed his coat. "We have to move fast," I said. "If we don't, the virus will have moved on and my heart will be nothing but a scar, if it isn't already at this point. Don't let them do a bunch of confirming tests. Just get the heart biopsy, so that we can start treating this right now. I know you are thinking about sending me to Children's Hospital— don't. They won't be able to do anything for me there. Send me straight to St. Paul's hospital."

He remained motionless with his head slightly tilted towards me so that his glasses hung farther down his nose. He ran his hand through his salt and pepper hair and seemed to be running through what I had just told him. "Did one of the other doctors talk to you already?" he all but whispered.

"No, no one has said anything to me at all."

He backed away, keeping his eyes on me and tried once more to make some kind of logical sense out of all this. "Did you hear the nurses talking about you?"

I just shook my head. A tear formed in the corner of my eye, and I realised for maybe the first time that maybe I wasn't going to be able to save myself after all. I was just a teen. No one listens to teenagers. A fear that had not gripped me since I was sixteen my first time seemed to fill every crevice in my body. I found myself shaking and I breathed deep breaths for fear of ripping out my IV. An alarm above my bed went off. My heart rate was going through the roof.

I had five people around me before I even knew what to think. A lot of muttered questions filled my ears, but it was like they were trying to all cram in at the same time and there was nothing intelligible that made it to my brain. Finally, my doctor took center-stage and made me focus on him. "Adam you need to relax. You need to calm down. Just breathe and relax, Adam."

I realized that I was holding my breath and I exhaled deeply. A worship song started playing in my head. Instruments and full choir voices started to take form. *Turn your eyes upon Jesus. Look full in his wonderful gaze. And the things of Earth will grow strangely dim, in the light of his glory and grace.* Soon I found myself almost to the point of complete relaxation. I closed my eyes and fell asleep.

The doctors and nurses around my bed shook me and called my name loudly. "Adam!"

I opened my eyes and looked around me. What was that? I had never remembered that happening to me the first time. The doctors looked at me confused but relieved that I was awake.

That afternoon they sent me by ambulance to St. Paul's. I was glad that someone had actually listened. My dad came with me, but before we left I told Mom to make sure he had taken his seizure medication. She didn't question me and made him go and get it before he came along for the ride. I wasn't about to have him have a seizure like he had the last time. Just before I left, my pastor and his wife came in to pray for me. I wished I knew what to tell them other than what they got at that moment, but honestly no one knew what was really going on, and as of right then I still felt I knew more than the doctors did.

They rushed me to the other hospital, and for the next two weeks they did every test known to them on me. I knew they were coming so I was ready for them this time. It seemed to shock some of the techs when I positioned myself where I needed to be without their direction. I received a lot of, "Have you done this before?"

I shook my head. The reality was that in this lifetime I had not, so I didn't feel like I was lying. That question always brought a twinge of guilt when I answered it.

I became newsworthy material. Someone had let it out that I had diagnosed myself before anyone had, that I somehow knew things that I shouldn't. They started calling me "the prophet patient." My friends got a kick out of it. My new nickname became PP, something that I didn't have last time either.

I found myself in my hospital room three weeks later when the doctors walked in and gave us the news. They were all very grim in their demeanours, and I knew that I wasn't expecting great news. The level of how bad the news was—now that is what I was waiting for. In my past I'd been told that by the time they had sorted everything out they were too late to catch the virus and it had left my heart mostly scarred and with only twelve percent heart function.

Now I waited to see what was going to happen. Was I truly able to change my life or like those who had developed cancer, would I just have to live out what was thrown my way?

The head doctor, in whom I was reminded as to why I had so strongly despised him the last time, cleared his throat. I don't know why exactly, but this man always grated me the wrong way. I'd ended up referring to him as Iggy the first time, and it seemed suitable even now. Iggy had hated the fact that I diagnosed myself, and instead of trying to find answers for me he seemed intent on proving me wrong. The look on his face right now proved two things to me. The first thing it proved was that I was right all along, the second, was that he hated being shown up by anyone.

My mom was tense and my dad sat silently.

"You have dilated cardiomyopathy, which means that your heart is…"

I tuned out because I knew the explanation and just sat there waiting until he was done. I had a huge smile on my face, and I think I was throwing him off a bit. I even laughed a couple times; really loving the chance to get under this guy's skin. I knew that I would be forced to see the shrink after this conversation, but I had seen her a few times and didn't mind messing with her mind either. He stumbled over his last couple of words, and then I stood up slowly and started clapping my hands in a standing ovation. "Good job! Great job everyone! Now that you've told me everything I told you when I first got here, can you please answer me this question? Did you or did you not catch the virus while it was still in the system?" Proud of myself and laughing my head off in my mind, I sat down and waited for an answer.

All of the doctors Iggy had chosen to parade in there with me were stunned. I don't know what they were thinking, but I knew I was having fun. A doctor from behind Iggy spoke up after a couple of minutes of silence and awkward glances between him and the other doctors. "We were able to catch the virus while it was still in your heart."

"Ok great. So I'm assuming you already have me on antibiotics. So my next question is, what is my heart function at? I remember listening very clearly to Dr. Ignozefski [Iggy] and heard no mention of heart function."

A different doctor cleared his throat from Iggy's other side. "Well that's the thing. If the meds work the way they should then we're looking at you most likely having a heart function of fifty to fifty-five percent."

Now normally that number would look really bad to most people, but I already knew from my past that the average person only has about sixty-five percent heart function. I started hooting and hollering. My mom and dad looked shocked because in their minds they'd just heard what should have been earth-shattering news for me. But I knew the truth! So that my parents would be in on this little celebration of mine, I asked the doctors, "Can you tell me what an average person's heart function is?" The doctors answered and still my parents seemed deeply worried that I sat there with an expression of *Hallelujah! Amen!* on my face. To live ten percent down from average was incredible to me. It was almost the complete opposite from my past where I was ten percent from death. Eleven percent is where they start prepping you for heart transplant. I knew what this news was, and to me it was almost just as good as them saying my heart was perfectly normal.

Iggy wouldn't let me have my moment though. "Mr. Adam," he said in a very grave voice, "this is a very serious situation you are in here. You have no idea how close you were to real trouble."

"Trust me, I did! That's why I'm so happy!"

Iggy seemed to have had enough of me and stomped off followed by his entourage, all with clipboards in hand. It took a while for me to explain to my parents that I wasn't insane and that this was the best news I had ever heard. They, for some reason, just didn't get it.

They kept me in there for another two days. A nurse came in and told me that I had strongly offended Iggy by being overly happy, and that he would not see me anymore because I was a waste of his precious time. I laughed. She continued to tell me that the medication had not only been able to get rid of the virus, but it had helped the heart heal to a complete seventy percent. I stopped her. I asked her if she had meant sixty-five percent. She shrugged her shoulders and told me that she had been informed that because of how much of an athlete I was, my heart was in extreme condition, and it was performing way higher than the average standard. I could not help but smile at this. I went home that evening, walking around with a heart that was better than average and friends waiting to see me again.

After the hospital I was given the chance to take the rest of the school year off. I refused. I was healthy and happy and wanted to not be stuck in a house that had nothing but questions. I was truly a mystery and I had people asking every question you could think of. When I was home at night I just closed my eyes and focused on my new question. *What do I do now?* I had stayed far from drugs and drinking. I couldn't bring myself to do anything with a girl. I was totally healthy and had pissed off Iggy more than I believe I could ever have in the past. *Now what?*

Grade eleven started soon and I had no idea what I was supposed to do now, so I just lived normal. Went to school like all my friends, laughed, and had fun. When I was walking down the hall one day, a face passed me that rang a bell in my head. I turned and stared at him as he walked away. His name was Brad. I knew him as a friend of a friend, but why was he jumping into my head so much? It was as if I was supposed to remember him for something he did. It was hard because some of the memories I had about school were so fuzzy and seemed to take a secondary place to my family and adult life. I remembered Alexander's first day of high school a lot better than I remembered mine. A smile broke across my face. I was going to live to see his graduation. Maybe I'd go for a second child this time.

I lost myself in thought in the middle of my school hall. It took me a while to remember what had caused me to stop in the first place. Brad. What was it about him that I needed to remember so much? The warning bell went and I realized that I was still far from class, so I quickly made my way to my psych class. I sat down, still bothered by Brad and what I was missing. The teacher started class by saying today's lesson was strictly dealing with emotional disorders, which included many forms of depression. Yet another alarm sounded off in my head. Brad and depression seemed to be two pieces of the same puzzle. I just didn't know how they fit.

A few days later while I was walking home from school, a journalist found me and wanted to ask some questions. He was from *Sci-Fi Monthly*. He was wondering if my ability to see the future was the result of some extensive anal probing. "Look, idiot," I said very annoyed "My heart issue was a fluke. I saw something on TV that made me freak…out…" Lying seemed to be the only way out of some of the constant questions.

All of a sudden the puzzle came together. Six months after my heart problem in the past, Brad had contracted the same thing. Only he'd died.

I was going to save him or at least try. I went to him at school the next day. "Hey Brad," I said from behind him. "How are you doing, bud?" I was generally nice to everyone so it wasn't too odd hearing me say anything like that to anyone. When he turned and faced me I knew that he was already sick. He didn't answer me but he seemed winded from just having climbed the stairs in the school. "Dude, are you feeling ok?" I asked, although I already knew the answer.

"I'm fine. Can I go now?"

I didn't know what to say without freaking him out too much. "Hey Brad, did you hear about my story? About how I knew I had something that the doctors didn't even know?"

"Yeah, I think everyone has heard that story, Adam."

"Well, what would you say if I told you I'm psychic, and one of my gifts is to see sick people?"

"That would be a crappy 'gift,'" he said, apparently not really wanting to know where this was going.

"Brad, you have the same thing I had, and you need to be seen by a doctor now."

He stood motionless for a beat then turned away from me and headed down the hall.

"It's called cardiomyopathy! Tell them to check your heart!" I called after him.

He never turned around, just kept going. I remembered when he had died it was really hard for me. I thought that his death was just foreshadowing what would happen to me. This was 1999—we were on the verge of Y2K and he died not long after.

In my new life, I didn't see him at school for a long time. We ran in different crowds normally, but when I looked for him or asked about him people just shrugged. Christmas break came up, and it was my happiest Christmas ever. I enjoyed every moment of it. We sang, we ate, and we were merry. I went back to school trying to find Brad or hear any news of him. It was odd because last time I'd been asked to counsel and to spend time with his younger brother. That never happened this time. I tried finding a picture of Brandon (Brad's brother) so that I could remember what he actually looked like, but that didn't help either.

I ended up going to the principal. She told me that he had indeed gone to the hospital and was told he had the same thing I did. The doctors were dismayed and a little concerned that I had been the one to point him to the hospital. He was in full recovery. The virus was caught right at the beginning of attacking the heart.

I got Brad's address from her and thought it would be good to see if he was home. I knew the area where he lived but not the exact house. Having the address from the school kind of pinned that down. I knocked on the door and really didn't know what to expect. I heard what sounded like a stampede of feet coming down the stairs. Brad opened the door as if expecting someone else, which he probably was. Then he realised who I was and grabbed me into a hug. "You saved my life!"

The remainder of my grade eleven year seemed to slip into obscurity. I had the odd phone call from far out magazines and after news I had saved Brad's life got out, I was constantly bombarded with people asking me if they were sick or dying. I had become somewhat of a celebrity. I tried to shy away from the limelight as much as I could, and after refusing countless people's requests for me to tell them of their future, things eventually got quiet.

The summer of grade eleven the church went to Mexico for a short-term mission trip. It was fun and exciting, and certain things that were in my mind proved to play out way differently this time. Still, they seemed to be small by comparison to the life I had just changed.

Grade twelve came and went. It was odd because I had taken an extra year to finish my schooling last time and this time I finished on time, with great marks. I was voted in as one of the valedictorians, which was something I had never even dreamed of last life. I hadn't even attended my ceremonies before. This time I got myself a grad date and did the whole experience. I decided that it was important this time around to feel like I had a sense of completion.

Fall 2001 was coming and I knew that the world, not just my life but the entire world was about to change. By August of that year I had already decided to make a count calendar of sorts. The same president was in office and I knew that by my actions I could not hold back the events that were to happen. In fact, I remembered clearly how much the States had freaked out the first time—how anyone and everyone that seemed to have any information to do with the events of that fall was put under a microscope. I decided that I would not put myself in that kind of situation. I would allow these things to happen; besides which, I wouldn't even know where to begin if I chose to inform people. I shrugged my shoulders in a sense and told myself that it wasn't my problem.

September 10th, 2001 and I found myself praying my butt off. "God, please be merciful," I prayed. I locked myself in my room and cried out to God. My mom found my actions odd and didn't understand what was going on. She knocked on my door a few times that day asking me if I was ok. At dinner that night I told my mom and dad that something really bad was going to happen the next day. Maybe it was the whole situation with my heart and how I seemed to know things that I shouldn't have known, but they didn't even bat an eye in my direction. They just both nodded their heads and asked what we should pray for. I told them to pray for New York. Pray for protection and for God to be where he needed to be.

September 11th, 2001: "Adam, you need to see this," my mom said.

I got out of bed and walked towards the TV. Just like last time, right in front of my eyes on a live feed from CNN, the second plane crashed into the second tower. I dropped to my knees and prayed. I felt like I was buried in sand up to my chest while the tide came in. The feeling wasn't of sadness or hurt but of overwhelming guilt. I could hardly breathe. My mom's eyes were glued to the set as she went about doing the dishes. She didn't know the magnitude of what was happening. The towers hadn't fallen yet. I sighed deeply and told myself there was nothing I could have done.

A breaking news story came in from a new location in the country. There was another plane down. I knew the Pentagon would be hit too, so I went and sat in the big comfy love seat so that my mom could see everything that was going on. *Nothing I could have done*, I kept saying.

Another news reporter from yet another location came on screen. "The White House has been hit," came the panicked voice of a female reporter, who had tears visibly running down her cheek. "I repeat…the White House has been hit by another plane…stay tuned for amateur video of the event."

WHAT!? I could not figure out what I had just heard. They went on to say that the president was safely in the air and that the vice-president was at Martha's Vineyard. The White House did not get hit the first time. I wasn't involved in any aspect of this event. Why had it changed? Had I done something? I remembered a theory that if a butterfly flapped its wings in China it would cause a hurricane in the States. Every little thing that we change has an effect on the world. Episodes of *The Simpsons,* in which Homer got his hands on a time machine and changed the present by accidentally killing a bug, or at one point all the dinosaurs, flooded my mind. I came to realize that maybe just something done differently this time may have had an effect, whether big or small on September 11th. More people dead. More damage done—the more hunger for revenge there was about to be.

"The First Lady, Laura Bush has been killed," the TV seemed to be booming. She had been in residence at the White House when the plane hit. The plane had done most of the damage to the residential side of the capital building. The news anchor didn't seem to know how to react. I don't blame the man; people were still reeling from the towers that were now just starting to collapse. I don't know what feeling must've been in him knowing that it was on his shoulders to tell the world that the First Lady had been killed. How history would see him as a messenger of death. I knew that the world would never be the same, and that a lot would be done in the name of bettering the protection of the states. I knew that like in the past, this day of unbelievable horror would come and go and that there would be so much that would happen that would be the theme and drive for many songs yet to come. History, I knew, would carefully watch the steps of all who led now, and I knew that nothing was to be solved through war and bloodshed. I was to stand back and watch the vengeance and let the world unfold much as it had before.

I decided that with all that was going on in the world at this point, to dedicate some time to helping others. My heart was always for helping teens, so I volunteered to answer phones at a youth crisis line. It was so difficult trying to explain to teens that although the world seemed dark and answers were not in sight, that things would be better. The hardest question for me to answer was why. I didn't have an answer for all the hatred that seemed to thrive in the world, and I found myself quickly being sapped of my strength. Even my extra years of experience seemed to fail me now.

Feeling burnt out, I sought God for a way of rebuilding the passion I once had. Going through my memories, I remembered the fun I'd had as a summer staff in Mexico and decided to pursue a discipleship through Youth With A Mission (YWAM). I love YWAM and wanted to pursue it again this life but fuller.

Something happened while on my outreach for the Discipleship Training School (DTS). I found that I was falling for one of the girls that were on the mission with me. She reminded me so much of my wife that I wondered when I first met her if she was. I had time before I first met my wife still, so I wondered if that meant it would be ok for me to see what this girl was all about. We were there first and foremost for God so we stayed focused as much as possible, but she easily caused me to lose that focus. I had those butterflies in my stomach and when she accidentally brushed my hand while reaching for a sandwich my entire body tingled. She made me feel the same way…the same way my…my wife. I couldn't remember my wife's smell anymore. I forgot the feel of her lips. Maybe this was what was supposed to happen now. Maybe DTS girl was supposed to be the one I was supposed to be with in the first place, and I'd ended up with my wife, from a past life. Was it a past life or was it this life? I don't know what my mind was thinking, all I know is that DTS (her name was Kim) was here and now. I knew Kim felt the same way. When I closed my eyes to sleep now, I didn't know if I dreamed of my wife or of Kim. I didn't know if I remembered the smell of my wife who seemed now so far away and just a memory, or if it was Kim's intoxicating fragrance that filled my senses.

One night, I made my way to the washroom and standing there waiting for the person who was using the single bathroom in the entire house was Kim. She stood there in a T-shirt that was more or less like a dress on her. She smiled at me as I made my way towards her and the bathroom. There was a twinkle in her eyes with every step I took closer. The dimple on her left cheek looked like a half moon. Her straight, dark-brown hair seemed to cascade over her shoulders. I paused and looked down at the ground in guilt. The hand with which she was nervously twisting curls in her hair dropped to her side, as she realised that for some reason I wouldn't move any closer. She took a step closer and then from behind her the bathroom door opened, and her roommate slowly examined the scene, "girl giggled," and rushed off to her room. I kept my distance and Kim turned to enter the bathroom.

I thought for a second to return to my room. Nature was cruel and I knew that I might not be able to risk a return trip. I moved towards the door and leaned up against the wall. *God, what am I supposed to do?* I asked myself. *I like her a lot God, but what about my wife?* I don't know why I said it out loud but quietly I said, "God, please give me a sign if you want me to romance Kim."

Just then the door to the bathroom opened and there stood Kim. A soft smile on her face, she brushed away the hair from in front of her face and tucked it in behind her ear. "Hi," she said so softly.

"Hi," I awkwardly said in return, still looking towards the floor.

All the awkward moments that hadn't been so awkward the second time were all being avenged in this one moment. My heart was pounding and my mouth was dry. I could feel my palms starting to get all sweaty. Even though I was leaning against the wall my knees seemed like they could no longer support my weight.

Then it happened. She touched me. She slightly placed her hand on my chin and raised it up so that I was looking into her deep brown eyes. She smiled and brushed my hair out of my face. "Why are you being so shy?" she asked.

"I don't know Kim; you just make me feel like no one ever has before."

Her smile widened, showing off her white teeth. She placed her hand flat on my cheek and moved in towards me. Her lips came so close to mine and there she just paused for the briefest of seconds, but it felt as though my lifetimes could have both been lived again in that pause. Then she kissed me. All the lame references in the world couldn't describe the feeling of her lips touching mine. Soft and tender at first and then as if knowing she had permission to continue there was no holding back the fullness of her kiss. I hugged her as we continue to kiss and nothing was left in my mind besides this woman who had totally captured my heart. I wanted no other than her.

I opened my eyes as if I'd been shot. Though still

locked in this kiss, my mind started racing towards my wife. Then it slammed the name *Alexander* into my view. I needed to stop and to stop now! Images of my wife came flooding into my head as if someone had just released the floodgates; scenes of our first kiss and first date and the moment I fell in love with her and the day my son was born. How beautiful she was in her wedding dress and how much she loved me even though I had screwed up many times by her. I was here cheating on her. I was kissing a girl that I didn't have a son with.

I pushed Kim away. "I'm sorry, I can't," I said as I turned away and made my way back to my room. The shame I felt from that night took a long time to fade. I was in my early twenties and still kept to myself in the area of romance and girls. I would not slip up like that again.

People I had been close to grew apart from me. I felt like it was more or less my fault this time. I wasn't interested in the lives they were leading. Parties and drinking were beneath me. I made the odd trip to the bar for a friend's birthday, but always chose to remain the sober one of the bunch. I had met new people that I couldn't wait to come around. Salina, who in my last life had become one of my dearest friends, made her first appearance at the church when I was nineteen. She came in and I don't know if it was because of my experiences with her already or what, but it was like I was able to pick up things with her exactly where I left them from before. We connected and she soon regained the position of dearest sister in my life. We were able to make each other laugh no matter when. We were both youth leaders together, and I found her to be someone I could totally be honest and open with. We had our moments of arguments, but we never let that get between us and our friendship.

The appearance of Salina brought to my life several people that I knew would end up being the most important people to me. I started to feel like the picture was starting to finally reveal itself yet again. I may have gone and changed some of the outcomes, but by just remaining in the church I found the people I loved and waited for those relationships to form again. The weird thing is many of them didn't. I was friendly with everyone, but there was something different this time around. I stayed away from the friends who had hurt me previously, and tried to stay closer to the ones who had proved in my past life that they were worth staying close to. I avoided those who brought nothing but anger and frustration, but in doing so I seemed to lose part of me. I had a strong relationship with God and had many friends, but part of me was still missing. I couldn't find or figure out what I needed.

I started to work for the church as a youth intern. I didn't make loads of money, so I took a job at a local restaurant. I got my licence and had my own car, whereas the last time around I didn't manage that until much later in life.

I worked at the White Spot for a couple of years. My life was filled with youth ministry and work. I found that the majority of the friends I had in school faded, and even my old church friends slowly stopped calling. Maybe they felt like I had become one of the judgemental church people who would judge them for their actions. Maybe I was. I had never had the problems with church like the first time around. I was seen as one who toes the party line. When most people tried to find things to complain about, my favourite quote ended up being, "Are you perfect?"

The chance I had to move out never happened the way it had the first time. I found myself trying to work more just to survive, and it was made apparent to me later that I needed to find a career that would support me well into old age. I decided to head to Bible college. It was something I had always wanted to do in both my lives but had never ended up doing for one reason or another. I took a pastoral course and invested all my savings into being a student. I was getting older now, and I had to face the fact that some of the people and experiences I had from my last life were now just memories. I saw the people I was close to at one time, but they were nothing but acquaintances. The only person that was the same in both lives was Salina. Even there things were different, though. She was the same but the way I felt towards her was odd. It was almost like I had walked through her problems with her once already, and to do it again felt like I was wasting my time.

Two of the most important friendships I'd had in my last life never happened this time around. I never got to know my roommate from my previous life; he had become one of my closest friends. I tried to find him and to befriend him, but he seemed like he wanted nothing to do with me. It may have been a chain reaction, but I also never grew close to another person who I dearly loved. For a time I had mentored him in my past life. We had first started hanging out with my one-time roommate, but this time, with no roommate in the picture we never seemed to connect. In both cases I tried as hard as I could, but it had seemed so easy and so seamless before. After being rejected by both of them numerous times I let them fade to memory. I mourned those friendships as if they were someone who had died in my life.

I moved out on my own later than I wanted to, this time to an apartment overlooking downtown Maple Ridge. It was very odd living six stories up instead of in a basement suite, where I had for so many years in my first chance. I finished my Bible college course and now knew that my life was truly about to start. The time was nearing when I first met my wife. I knew when and where and I would do everything possible to make sure that it came true.

The closer the day came, the more I heard her voice in my mind. I could see her face with my waking eye. I smelt her perfume in every hallway and elevator. I was a man obsessed. I got in my car on the day and put my seat belt on. My heart was pounding so hard that I felt like it was now a curse to have a heart with a function that was better than average. I hadn't even put the keys in the ignition, and I had sweat marks on my shirt. I put my hands on my lap and took a deep breath. *Calm down Adam. It's just the love of your life. You know her. Don't be nervous.*

I started up my car and headed out of the parking garage. The entire way there seemed to be nothing but corny love songs on the radio. From Whitney singing that she would always love you to when a man loves a woman. I turned it off and just prayed the rest of the way. I arrived at Canada Place in Vancouver faster than I'd thought I would. Feeling unprepared, again I started to worry. I said a silent prayer, got out of my car, and walked into Missions Fest with a mission of my own. I walked to where I remembered seeing her for the first time. There was a bench, so I sat. It must've looked odd, me just sitting there waiting to see her.

An hour went by and nothing. I wasn't sure what time it had been when I'd met her exactly, but I was ok with waiting. I had waited twenty-eight years for this one moment. I could wait just a little more. People I knew walked by and recognized me. They came by and said hi. I was trying to keep my eye on the hall. I didn't mean to be rude but my friends walked away a little rejected, and I made a mental note to make it up to them later. Three hours went by, and then on the overhead speaker closing time was announced. My heart began to sink. Where was she!? *Did I do something wrong here? Did I go to the wrong area?*

I made my way to my feet and defeated, I slowly walked to the exit nearest my car. What had happened? I pushed the heavy glass door open and a hand gently tapped my shoulder. "Excuse me?"

I paused. I knew the voice. I knew who it was who stood behind me. I swallowed hard and let out the breath that had been captured at the sound of her voice.

"I think you dropped this."

I turned and standing there in front of me was this dark-haired beauty. Her face wore a gentle smile, and her eyes were dark and deep just as they had been. "Hi Adam," she said.

"Kim, um, it's nice to see you again."

She heard the disappointment in my voice and simply handed me my hat, which I had truly dropped back at the bench. "Yeah, nice to see you too." Her eyes spoke for her. They looked as they had the night I'd walked away from her in the hall. Like I had once again told her that I didn't want her.

I tried to smooth things over but couldn't find any words worth saying. I remained silent as she went on to be somewhat pleasant in trying to catch me up with what was going on in her life. I started to venture off into my own thoughts trying to figure out if I had the wrong year or if maybe I had come on the wrong day. But I was sure. I was more certain of this than I had been of anything I had ever been.

"So yeah, what's new with you?" Kim asked, snapping me back into the present.

I told her that I was looking for someone and that I hadn't found her. Kim looked at me like I was nuts for not trying to call this person's cell. I didn't know how to say that I didn't even "know" her. I knew her—just didn't know her.

Kim and I parted after an awkward goodbye and an even more awkward hug. I sat in my car with tears in my eyes and banged the dash cursing loudly. This was the moment! I put my head on my steering wheel and cried. That night I drove home with utter defeat as my companion.

Walking through the door of my apartment that night, I left a trail of keys and coat and hastily kicked off shoes in my wake as I landed face first in my couch. Totally zapped of any energy, I felt as if I had just run a marathon. Tears began to burn again at my eyes and the whispers of failure seemed to echo through my mind. I moved to sit on my couch in complete darkness with my hands holding my head. Light from the patio seemed to melt into my world but just out of reach of where I sat. I could not believe the metaphors that were running through my mind at that moment. Not being able to answer the questions I had burning in my mind, I found myself just sitting there waiting for something to make sense again. The night seemed to linger.

By the time sunlight started to peek over the mountains on the horizon, I had come to a decision that I wouldn't just allow this woman, whom I loved so much, to just disappear. I remembered telling Alex years ago that if there was something worth loving than it was worth fighting for. That if we never fought for the things we loved then how could we call ourselves worthy of that love? My next actions seemed desperate to me, even a little crazy, but it's out of our desperation that sometimes the greatest things in our lives happen. I decided to hunt down my wife—to find her and to arrange for me to be somewhere she was.

I went online and Googled her name. In my haste I had actually been stupid enough to put down her married name, my last name. The results came up and I found total and utter disbelief when at first I saw no mention of her. Upon seeing my mistake the fear that grew in me like an overwhelming tide seemed to subside as my hope yet again started to burn in my soul. Deleting the previous search, I typed in Stephanie Charity Williams. Before I hit the return button to start my search I took a deep breath and swallowed hard, hoping to cleanse that last bit of fear before I headed into the unknown. I hit enter and my computer went to work, slowly bringing up the search results. The page rebooted and there was nothing. The screen went to the warning screen that said that Internet Explorer had stopped working. My connection was dead. I refreshed the screen, and again there was the same blue taunting page standing in the middle of the screen and telling me of my most recent failure. I restarted my computer and impatiently waited for all the common set-up features to take place. I didn't even realize that I had started to pace back and forth in front of the computer until I saw my start-up page waiting for me to log on. I sat down again, brought up Internet Explorer and headed to Google again. Again I put in her name and stared viciously at the screen, daring it to fail me again. There it was. Her name or at least one of many people that held the same name she had. I skimmed them as I went looking for her. I came across one that just spoke of her and wondered if it was her, but I didn't see anything that held her picture or anything that I was familiar with. I racked my mind for things I had been told about her past like what schools she attended or some things she was interested in when she was younger. Panning page after page that might have something to do with her, I held my breath. Stephanie seemed to be a ghost. I finally tried looking up her parents and found that they were living in Michigan and that they had been there for years. Something was already wrong. The Stephanie I knew was born and raised in Washington State, and yes we had met at Mission Fest in Vancouver but she had been visiting a friend that weekend and they'd decided to take it in.

I found the contact number for her parents and phoned them, telling them a lie about being a friend of Stephanie's from high school and that I was trying to get a hold of her. Even just hearing her mother's voice brought flooding memories of the toast she said over Stephanie and I on our wedding day. I could see her face, which was so similar to my Stephanie's. Steph's mom told me that she was in Vermont and that she didn't feel comfortable giving me her number because my name didn't ring a bell with her. She offered to pass my number to her daughter but I decided that would be really hard to explain to both Stephanie and her mother, it being a Canadian number and an unknown person. I thanked my one-time mother-in-law and kindly told her that I would try another way. Maybe that might have sent up a warning especially since she was a really wise woman, but I thought that it would be a good enough cover for now.

I went to an online directory of Vermont, looked up Steph's name, and finally found a trace of my wife. On a complete whim of an urge I decided to book off the week and called work that morning so that I could go and find her.

I landed in Vermont really early in the morning. There was frost on the windows as I walked down the arrival ramp. The air was crisp and held a sweeter smell than home. I got to my car rental place relatively easily and found myself in my reserved hotel room no less than a quarter of an hour later. I felt foolish now that I was there. I sat in my room realizing that all I was doing was following a memory. I was chasing ghosts. I took in the appearance of my one- bed, squared room, which seemed to be something out of a horror movie in the early seventies. Tacky yellow-flowered drapes hung over the one window in the room and a constant drip could be heard from the tap in the bathroom. *What am I doing here? She doesn't even know me. I'm nobody to her and yet she's everything to me.* She was everything to me. I argued with myself for hours, sometimes seated on the foot of the well-used bed, while other times I found myself perched on the edge of the grime-covered tub tracing the grout with my eyes as I debated my situation. I finally decided that there would be no harm in at least going to the address I had for her. I had already paid for the hotel, plane, and rental, so I might as well go and see if I could see her, maybe even talk to her.

It was just after noon now and I was feeling the same way I had when I went to see her at Missions Fest earlier in the year. Thanks to Mapquest, my job in finding her address was easier than I wished it was. It could always be a reason for fate not allowing me to see her...I got lost and never found her house. But with the world's technology I had been given a direct path to her house.

I drove by her address three times. Up one way then back. I noticed neighbours taking notice of me. Maybe I was kind of looking a little suspicious, but in my mind it was worth it. I parked a few houses down from hers and just sat there. I was hoping to see her; to get a glimpse of her. I lost track of time half-watching people walk by and half-continuing my ongoing debate in my mind.

Tap, tap, tap. I was deep in thought as the window next to me was now the only barrier between me and the invader of my thoughts. I turned with a look of one who was frustrated but confused at the same time. I lowered the glass divider, expecting to see the face of a police officer. The sun was just starting to set now and the face of the one in front of me was partly shadowed. I let my eyes adjust and there in front of me was a pair of the darkest brown eyes I've ever seen. These eyes I knew though. There was no mistaking the gaze of the person I was now only inches from. Her skin was olive and her hair was longer than I had ever seen it. Her brow was frowned, but the loveliness of her face still melted away any doubt in my mind. "Excuse me," she said, "I don't know if you know this but this is a family-oriented neighbourhood, and you, sir, are kind of creeping everyone out."

I stumbled for my words, which in retrospect may have been an admission of some kind of slight guilt in her eyes.

"If it wouldn't put you out too much, I was hoping

that you would be on your way."

I sat there wide-mouthed and shocked. Stephanie had always been such a straightforward and blunt person. I had often had her scorn directed at me throughout our life together and wasn't shocked, but the anger and slight fear behind her voice told me that I had outworn my welcome. "I'm sorry. I didn't mean to scare anyone. I just needed a place to think for a little bit."

I started my car and turned again to Steph. Then I looked down and noticed that she was no longer my Stephanie. On her wedding finger sat a diamond ring and a golden band. She was married.

"I'm sorry," I said one more time and drove off.

I found myself at a loss in my hotel room the next morning. I had just come here to find that my wife, my completion, the one that I was to marry and to bring my son Alexander into the world with. She was now and forever gone to me. I was beyond tears. I had lived my life with the expectation that I would get to fall in love with her all over and have the joy of making and holding Alexander once more. I had lived my life to better myself for them. I wanted to be there for Alex's huge events, and now not only would I never see him attend his graduation or wedding, he would never exist. All my goals and driving forces in life seemed to have in one moment just disappeared. I turned to God in prayer. *What are you doing to me here?* seemed to be an ongoing question that popped up several times in that prayer. This was supposed to be my life over and I did it over; I played along but you changed the rules on me! I served you with everything I had this time around! I didn't party or smoke and drink—I was the model Christian! And here I am in a room in Vermont slowly losing the desire to even stand. I found myself tired and physically unable to stand so I passed out, not knowing how I made it to my bed or when I took off my clothing.

I was brought back into the world by a gentle tap on the door. "Hello, I need to clean the sheets." After throwing my clothes back on I got up and answered the door. "I could come back later," said the older woman who was pushing along her maid cart.

I was surprised that this room had ever been cleaned let alone had a maid service. I told her that I was hungry and would be leaving for breakfast so that she could have access to the room. I gathered everything of importance that I would need for the next few hours and headed out. It was much later than I had thought. By the time I made it to the cafe on the corner of the downtown street it was already pushing noon. It was nice weather and good for walking so I grabbed coffee and a bagel and egg sandwich, which they named a beggall, and headed towards a park that was suggested by the young cashier. There was no playground at the park, it was just fields of rolling green with a baseball diamond in one of the far-off sides. The panoramic view would have been breathtaking had I been in a train of thought that was less introverted. I had one more day before my return trip was scheduled. I thought that I would maybe need this amount of time to find a chance to talk with Stephanie. The thought of returning home wasn't high on my list of things I was looking forward to, especially since I'd left without rhyme or reason. I doubted I could explain it to anyone. I still needed to figure that one out.

As I ate my meal a young boy ran past. My heart lurched as from the corner of my eye he looked so similar to Alexander that I had to strain to make out the differences between their faces. To my left came the rustling of someone's clothing and I turned to see the source of the noise. There stood Stephanie staring at me. I took it she had seen me staring intently at the mystery boy and had grown nervous because of my reaction. "Well, if it isn't you again." There was bitterness in her tone and apprehension. "You following us now?" she asked in her well- known sceptical voice.

I had a mouthful of beggall at the moment, so I just shook my head in fierce denial. I couldn't find the moisture in my mouth to swallow, so I spat out the food and cleared my throat.

"Look, I don't know who you are, but I'm having a really hard time believing that this is a coincidence." She paused. "Who are you? Why are you here?"

You'd think that for a man who had now lived two

lives I would know exactly what to say to her, but every scenario in my mind seemed to end up bad for me.

She sat down next to me. "Listen, if there's something you want to tell me then I think that for all parties involved here you'd better tell me before I call the cops and you can tell them." She now wore the face and tone that I knew meant she'd had enough of me. It seemed odd because really I hadn't done anything. I carefully thought about my words because I knew they could condemn me. "Do you believe in second chances?" I asked.

She looked at me in utter confusion. I wanted to hold her and tell her that everything would be okay—that I was her husband in a different life and that we were madly in love and had a son.

As I started to speak the boy ran by again and yelled at her to get her attention. "Mom! Watch me! I can do a handstand!"

"Not now Alex, Mommy's busy."

I couldn't say anything. His name was Alex? Who had stolen my life from me? "His name, is Alex…?" I all but whispered.

"Yes, I've always loved that name," she said in love and care as she turned to him as if she had forgotten everything that was happening between us. She gently shook her head and resumed her glare at me. "Don't change the subject," she said, shaking her head softly.

"My name is Adam," I started, "I don't know you and I

don't know your son. It's just all been a case of wrong place in the wrong time. I didn't mean to scare you or make you feel threatened by my presence. If you remember clearly I was seated when you and your son came here. I don't want to cause any trouble."

She examined me up and down and there was almost a sigh of relief that was visible in her body. "I'm sorry. Since his father left us I've been a little too over-protective."

I remembered that one of the qualities Steph had was that she easily trusted and shared her life with anyone. She seemed so hurt and damaged. What in life had caused all this pain that my Stephanie never expressed? My heart was so torn for her. "I'm sorry your husband left you and your son. That can't be easy." The fact that I had in ways done the same to her already in a previous life seemed to pound in my head. I'd left her and Alex already. But the boy that stood now just a few paces away was not my Alex. He was a handsome boy and shared similarities to my son, but this boy was the product of another person and didn't have the same smile, nor did he have the same look in his eye. This boy had a face that was rounder than my boy's. His eyes were lighter, almost unbelievably sky-blue. They would have passed as brothers easily, but I knew that would never happen.

She made to get up and the look in her eye told me that she was sorry, I nodded in return and she and her

Life After Death

son walked away from me across the field towards the parking lot near the baseball diamond. She turned back to look at me once from across the field. I did not see longing in her dark eyes—all I saw were questions and disbelief. This Stephanie wasn't the same person I'd fallen in love with. She was a broken, hurt person who had walls so thick that I would need a lifetime just to gain her true trust. The hope of regaining my life slowly marched away with every step she and Alex took.

I boarded my plane and headed home. Upon landing I came to realize that even though I'd had a very talkative neighbour the entire flight, I had said nothing. I was shuttled to my car and started the trip home. My mind went to Kim and how I had lost that chance for whatever possible future I may have had with her to hold out for my wife. I was almost thirty now and had waited my entire life for Stephanie, and now here I was in my car with nothing to show for anything in my life. I turned on my phone after my five days of being incommunicado to see that both my voice mail and my texts were full to the brim. I started with my texts because I was in no mood to hear any voices at that exact moment. The texts proved to be nothing of extreme import except for one from a friend to inform me that his wife was now expecting. That, if anything, broke my heart more than lifted me with excitement. I put in my phone headset and started to drive back home. I checked my voicemail and heard one from my mom asking about where I was, and there was one from Salina with a very similar tone of displeasure and concern in it. The third turned out to be a telemarketer. The next two were from my parents and I just ignored them once I realised that they were the same as the first. I had left a note on my door telling everyone that I would be gone for five days. Had they gone and looked they would know that I was safe. The ninth message confused me to the point that I thought they had the wrong number. It was a voice I couldn't place. All it said was thank you very much. My tenth and final message was from my mom. I was about to delete it but decided to let it play so that I could gauge the level of the anger I would be dealing once I called her.

There was a pause on the phone as the message started to play. Then, as if through tears, my mom's voice could be heard. "Adam, it's really important that you call. Dad has had a severe seizure, and we're not sure how bad the damage is. He's still in a coma. Call me , please."

I waited for the time and date to play and then guilt hit me hard. The message was from two days ago. I frantically called home, almost dropping my phone in the process. My eyes must've been off the road for less than a few seconds, and by the time I turned them back to the road it was too late.

"And so here you sit. Well that's the gist of it. It sounds almost unbelievable." The voice that was talking to me now was rich with youth. It wasn't a young person's voice but just filled with youth, piss, and vinegar.

I laughed as he seemed to look at me as if I was crazy. "If you think it's hard to believe can you imagine what I'm thinking about all this?" I examined his face to realize that instead of pity or a look of condemning craziness, his expression was almost jolly and utterly understanding.

I was sitting on the bank of a wide river. For some time I had been walking along a path that was made of a fine dust that glimmered in the sun with every step. I had heard the sound of the water running by in the distance and decided that I would seek out its source. It was green here. Trees were all around me but not in a suffocating sense. It was open and airy. There was a light all around that left no room for shadow.

My companion just seemed to be with me by the time I sat down. I regained my senses about me after realizing that I had been doing nothing but staring at this man's face for the last several moments. I looked towards the running water and glanced about me for a stone to skip. "So what now?" he asked.

Not knowing the answer I shrugged and spotted the stone I was seeking. I stood up and launched the stone into the water only getting two skips.

"Is that all?" the man laughed. He picked up one and sailed it across the surface of the water skipping it too many times for me to count. "What's your name?" he asked.

"My name…" I paused and then looked at him. "I think you already know that don't you?" I replied in a half mocking tone.

"Well, that depends," he said. "Who do you think I am?"

Every aspect of me knew that this was my Jesus. The Lamb of God, Jehovah, I am. "Well you're no prophet." I smiled. "Considering you don't even know my name."

He stood now and there was a smile in his eyes as he grabbed my shoulders and said, "Was that too obvious a question?"

I dropped to my knees and fell at his feet. "You're Jesus." I felt like I was yelling out the truth so that everyone could hear.

"Adam, you're already in Heaven. I'm pretty sure everyone here knows that." He grabbed me by the shoulders and brought me to stand again. "You have questions for me don't you?" he asked.

"Yes, a lot," was the only answer that seemed to work in the situation.

He smiled again and started to walk away from me. "Follow me," he said.

Who was I to refuse a simple command like that? I followed him and he led me to a green and rolling field identical to the park in Vermont, minus the baseball field. Far off in the distance beyond the open field a chorus was singing, and if I strained myself I could make out the words, "Turn your eyes upon Jesus."

I looked quizzically towards Jesus and he smiled.

"Keith Greene is leading the choir today."

I nodded; I was expecting hymns or songs I had not heard before. This was a nice surprise to me.

"One day I'll get you to lead it. I love your worship," Jesus said.

I was dumbstruck with complete surprise. Having other pressing matters in my mind, though, I shook it off and followed Christ to where a blanket had been set up. It looked like one of those picnics from a commercial with bright bold colours and a loving family and a dog that often ends up with the child with a grass stain for the mom to prove the power of Tide.

We sat and he opened the basket and handed me some bread. I couldn't help but notice the irony in it. As if reading my mind, which I wasn't sure if he could or not, Jesus gave me a look of disbelief hidden beneath a grin, and he shook his head. He handed me a cup and poured me some liquid. I was expecting wine and again he looked at me, but this time it was with an expression of slight humour as if to say, "Ha ha." We ate in silence for a bit. The bread was warm and light as if there was a bakery in the basket. The beverage was like nothing I've ever had. It was sweet and airy, and when it first hit your tongue it tasted sweet like honey but as it progressed further along the tongue the taste seemed to change. It ignited all the different taste buds in my mouth in a way that wasn't at all displeasing, but as if I had never truly tasted anything before. When again I bit into the bread it seemed to me that there were new flavours I had missed the first time. Although I knew there was no butter it was there. It tasted like meat as well, almost like a roasted beef—the most amazing and truly unique flavours I've ever tasted.

Jesus waited for me to fully enjoy the new sensations. "You have never truly tasted before, Adam," he said.

I didn't really understand but at the same time I knew fully what he meant by saying that. Again it took me longer than I thought, but I realized that I had questions. I put down my cup and bread and cleared my throat.

"Good—about time," Jesus said with a smile.

I don't know how, but I knew he was completely joking. "Why did you let me go back and live two lives?" I asked him.

Jesus looked at me and then said something that made me confused. "Why don't you tell me?"

I couldn't figure that one out at all. Why would he say that now that I was dead and there was nothing more to learn, except why he had allowed me, and apparently only me, to repeat life?

"What did you learn?" Jesus prodded.

My mind caused everything to rush through my eyes as if in fast-forward. I thought of how I had really messed around with my parents as a baby and sent the bullies running while I was in my grade-school years. I thought of my friendships and of all the things I had accomplished in his name. Then, like a truck going over a steep edge, my mind tumbled down to one conclusion. This had all been a stupid lesson. This was God's way of teaching me something that was pointless now that I was in Heaven. "This was all to teach me the moral of the story?" I more or less stated, rather than asked. "You let me go back and live my two lives so that I could learn that…I don't know what you wanted me to learn. All I know is that I feel more confused now than I did before."

"Why are you confused, Adam?" Jesus asked in his loving way.

"This doesn't happen often does it? Allowing your children to live their lives twice? So if I'm among a select few, then the question; what were you trying to show me? Maybe confused is the wrong word. I just don't understand your purpose."

"I can answer that, Adam Jason." After taking off some fruit that had been laid on it, Jesus passed me a silver platter and told me to look at my reflection. I took the platter and stared at it, expecting to see the twenty-eight-year-old me staring back, but in the mirrored surface the face that looked back on me was that of the forty-eight-year-old man who had died with his family at his side.

"What you see now Adam is the Adam who came to Heaven. You arrived here right after you closed your eyes on that hospital bed and haven't left here since."

I made to say something, but Jesus lifted his hand to stall anything that might have come out of my mouth. He continued, "Adam, you had a life that was hard to live. You had been given a huge trial in your life from a very early age on. I want you to know before I continue that I cried every tear you did. My heart broke every time yours did. I didn't want you to be in pain. I love you and I will reward you, because you were faithful to me in your pain and hurt. You continued to call out to me in your fear, and I love you so much for that. In our conversations you often asked me what if. What if you hadn't had a heart problem? What if you could send someone back to warn the past-you of the mess ahead of you? Why did you have to go through this?" He paused. "Your weak physical heart gave you great strength in your spiritual one. People were drawn to you and felt comforted by you because you had an understanding about fear and trials that most people never grow to understand. Cardiomyopathy became a tool and a weapon for my purpose, in which I used you to touch the lives of so many people, even if only in passing. I allowed you to play the "what if" game because I love you. I let your mind go and think that it was reliving your life so that you could see what would happen. I wanted you to be able to live here without those doubts in your heart. I gave you that chance to change your life."

Crestfallen, I said, "Yeah, I had the chance, but I ended

up losing everything that was of any real importance to me. I lost my wife and my son. I even lost some of my closest friends because I chose differently this time around."

"You found yourself unknowingly less compassionate and less kind and comforting, because you didn't live a life that taught you how to have those qualities. In fact, you became self-obsessed and focused merely on the goals you had for your own personal life. Before, you had put people before yourself almost without even thinking about it," Jesus said in a correcting voice.

"So I did nothing good and I lost all my loved ones."

"I didn't say you did nothing good. You just led a different life."

I hung my head down wishing that I hadn't had the chance to have a do-over. Then I stopped feeling sorry for myself and looked back at Jesus who was already smiling at me. It must have looked funny to him, because I could even feel my face change in all but slow motion as I realized that maybe I hadn't messed up so badly. "Did you say that you let my mind go and experience the "what if" game?" I asked my saviour.

He simply nodded his head.

"So Stephanie is my wife and Alexander is my son? And those last twenty-eight years were just a figment of my thoughts and imagination?"

Again Jesus nodded; this time with a huge smile on his face that broke into a laughter that brought my heart into joy. Relief surrounded me and I joined in his laughter. Finally I understood everything. We both quieted down after a good few minutes. Jesus sipped from his cup and I looked out to the distant horizon. "I miss them." Jesus placed his hand on my shoulder. "I miss them so much."

What was once laughter had turned into sadness until Jesus stood and looked down on me. "You know, the Bible says something about no tears of sorrow in heaven."

I sniffed liked a five-year-old and wiped my nose with my hand. Standing up, I bowed my head and said sorry. He just smiled and reassured me that they would be here sooner than I could imagine. He told me that there was so much for me to see in Heaven and that I would be guided by my very own angel.

I felt sad that I would be unable to be guided by my King, but I understood that he must be a busy man. He grabbed my shoulders and kissed my forehead. Softly he told me that I was loved and that everything was going to be ok. He then placed his hand on my chest. "This is your new body."

I looked down and saw that I was dressed in pure white robes that seemed to glow, but then I realized that it wasn't my clothing glowing, but me. I was glowing. I picked up the platter again and looked into the mirror and there before my eyes was me, but not me. I had lost age in my face, but I knew that it was still me. My eyes were bright blue and my teeth were brilliantly white. All the scars and imperfections I'd had on my face were no longer there. I looked at my neck to see the scar from when I was three, and it too was gone. Then I checked to see where they had opened up my chest, where they had placed in me a new heart. That scar was gone as were all the others I once carried. I was made whole again.

I looked around and noticed that I was now standing next to a man in a white gown that was glowing. I turned to him and realised that I was shining brighter than he was. "Are you my angel guide?" I asked.

He nodded his head, told me his name, and suggested a good place to begin. As we were about to take off I turned back towards the river where I'd been sitting, and there on a bridge I saw Jesus. I yelled out, "Goodbye Jesus!" feeling kind of like a kid the first time his parents leave him at kindergarten.

He looked straight at me and smiled, showing all of his joy. As clear as day and as if he stood right in front of me he said, "Welcome home."

At that moment, the memories of my wife and son and of all those who had been in my life poured into my mind, as if Jesus had unlocked my memories and allowed me to have the ones I cherished most be as if they had happened days prior. I smiled at the first time I had met my brother and at the family camping trips, which had birthed in me the joy of the outdoors. I held back tears of joy as I remembered the faces of my loved friends, who had held me up in my life when I couldn't hold on to God, and times of deep conversations that lasted deep into the morning hours, and hours of laughing for no apparent reason other than to just laugh. My parents who had sacrificed so much of their lives to ensure that I would live a life filled with love. Seeing my Stephanie for the first time and the moment I knew I had fallen in love with her. Holding Alexander and whispering a song to him that I knew came only from God, drying his tears, and hearing his laughter. My life unfolded in my mind's eye and for the first time in a very long time I felt complete.

The End.

CPSIA information can be obtained
at www.ICGtesting.com
Printed in the USA
LVOW08s0845090317
526600LV00001B/5/P

9 781460 297353